Tracking

by

Gill Harvey

Illustrated by Martin Remphry

For Jessica Virdee
MR

First published in 2008 in Great Britain by
Barrington Stoke Ltd
18 Walker Street, Edinburgh, EH3 7LP

www.barringtonstoke.co.uk

ISBN: 978-1-84299-517-4

Printed in Great Britain by Bell & Bain Ltd

Contents

Chapter 1
Camping Out

The sun had gone down, and the woods were growing dark. The last blackbird had stopped calling. It was so still that you could hear it when a tree branch creaked. The only other sound was the hiss of the little camping gas cooker, which was heating up some water for tea. Jamie and Ed lay in their sleeping bags just inside the front flap of their tent, watching the gas flame.

Suddenly, there was a scream, right above their heads.

"Wahhhh!" Both Jamie and Ed jumped.

Just in time, Jamie looked up, and saw something white flying off between the trees. "Only a barn owl," he said.

Ed shook his head. "I didn't see it," he said.

"You shouldn't need to see it," Jamie told him. "You should know what a barn owl sounds like!"

"Yeah, yeah," said Ed.

They settled down to watch the flame again for a few minutes.

Then Jamie poked Ed. "You were scared," he said.

Ed punched him on the arm. "So were you!"

Jamie grinned, and punched him back. "I was surprised," Jamie said. "That's not the same thing as being scared."

"Whatever." Ed reached to turn off the gas flame. The water in the kettle had started to bubble. "Right. Where are our mugs?"

The two boys were finishing their tea when Jamie heard another noise. Much closer this time, just behind the tent.

"What's that?" he said in a whisper.

"What?"

Jamie put a finger to his lips, and pointed. Both boys sat very still. There was something out there. They could hear it. And it was making a strange snuffling sound, very close to the back of the tent. The boys looked at each other.

"What d'you think it is?" asked Ed.

"Don't know," Jamie shook his head.

The sound stopped. Jamie started to creep forward. He peered round the flap of the tent,

but then there was a huge growl, and a big
shadowy creature jumped out of the
darkness.

"Wahhhhh!" The boys yelled.

The big creature began to laugh. "Got
you!"

It was Jamie's godfather, Sam.

"Sam!" Jamie was really angry. "What are
you doing here?"

Sam put his back-pack down. "Hey! Thanks for the welcome," he said. "If you must know, they let me off work, so I thought I'd come and join you."

He pulled a little tent out of his back-pack, and began to put it up. Even though it was dark, it only took him a few minutes. It was Friday night. The plan had been for Jamie and Ed to camp on their own just for one night – now they were 15 years old, their parents thought they'd be able to look after themselves. Sam was supposed to join them the next morning, but they didn't mind him showing up early. In fact, they were pleased.

He was an expert tracker, and could tell you about all the wild-life that had passed by, just by looking at the ground and all the plants. He was amazing at tracking people, too. He'd taught Jamie and Ed almost everything they knew about living in the woods.

LEARNING TO TRACK

To be a good tracker, you need to be aware of all the little things left behind by the humans and animals as they pass by.

- Bits of fur, hair or feathers

- Branches that have been nibbled by an animal feeding

- Droppings (poo), known as 'scat'

Sam set up a little lamp outside his tent. Then he pulled a big bag of marshmallows out of his back-pack, and three forks. "We can toast these on the gas flame," he said. "Not quite the same as a real fire, but close enough."

"Great!" said Ed. "I wish we could have a real fire, though."

"No way, not in these woods," said Sam. "We're lucky they've let us camp here, like this, rather than on a camp site."

Jamie lit the gas flame again. He stuck a marshmallow on a fork. Toasting marshmallows was one of the best bits about camping. You held one over the flame until the outside went a bit black and crispy. You pulled the crispy bit off and ate it. Yum. Then you put the rest of the marshmallow over the flame again to toast the next bit.

"So how did you find us, Sam?" asked Ed. "We thought we'd camped in the middle of nowhere."

"That's a stupid question," said Jamie, his mouth full of marshmallow. "He's a tracker. How do you think he found us?"

Ed punched Jamie's arm. "It's not stupid," he said. "Look round. It's totally dark out there."

"It's a good question, Ed," said Sam. "But you should be able to answer it by now."

"I guess you could hear us miles off," said Ed.

Sam nodded. "Yes. Noise travels in the woods. More than ever at night. But I did have a little bit of help." He fished in his back-pack again and took out a torch. He turned it on.

"A green light!" said Jamie. "Let's have a look!"

Sam passed the torch to Jamie. He trained the light on the ground and found one of his own foot-prints. It was amazing how much you could see in the green glow of the torch – all the little ruts and shadows.

GREEN LIGHT

A green light shows up tracks in the dark much better than an ordinary light. Also, it doesn't spoil human night vision the way an ordinary light does.

The barn owl gave another screech. This time, no one jumped. Jamie and Ed grinned at each other. With Sam there, the woods didn't seem scary. And anyway, there was nothing to be scared of. There weren't any bears or wolves or lynxes out there. There were only deer and foxes and badgers.

Nothing to be scared of at all.

Chapter 2
The Challenge

The sound of sizzling bacon woke Jamie up. He poked his head out of the tent. Sam was sitting on a log, cooking.

"Good morning!" he said. "Ready for some breakfast?"

"What time is it?" Jamie could just about see the sun rising between the trees.

"It's late. 6:30." Sam grinned at him. "You'll never be a good tracker if you don't learn to get up before the sun rises."

Jamie heard Ed groan too. But the bacon did smell really good. Then Sam cracked some eggs into the frying pan, too, and they began to gurgle and pop in the fat. Maybe getting up wasn't such a bad idea after all. Sam's camping breakfasts were famous. Somehow, he could cook bacon, eggs, mushrooms and tomatoes all on one little gas cooker.

Once they'd wiped their plates clean with chunks of crusty bread, Jamie and Ed washed up using hardly any water. They finished their tea. Then they felt ready to get started on a long day of tracking.

"Right," said Sam. "I'm going to set off that way." He pointed into the woods. "That's north-west. I want you two to wait for half an hour, then follow my tracks. Take it slowly. Check out what else is around. Make a note of all the wild-life as you go. I want you to find me by lunch-time."

Jamie and Ed nodded.

"Sounds great," said Ed. "We'll find you in no time."

"That's what you think!" said Sam, with a smile. "Well, I'll have to make sure I make it difficult for you!"

He picked up his bag and stick, then padded into the woods. Jamie and Ed watched him go. In a few moments, he'd vanished in between the trees.

While they waited for half an hour to pass, the two boys packed their own tracking bags. They didn't need much. They each had a pair of binoculars to look at things far away, and a magnifying glass to look at things up close. They had note pads and pencils, to make a record of any tracks that they found. They also had a compass in case they got lost, and hunting knives, which could be useful for all sorts of things. And lunch. It wouldn't do to forget lunch.

"I'm ready," said Ed, picking up his tracking stick.

TRACKING STICKS

A tracking stick is like a walking stick, with a point at one end for poking things. It also has little rubber bands rolled on to it. You use it like this:

When you find a foot-print, mark each end of it with a rubber band. This gives you the size of the print itself.

Next, mark the gap between that print and the next one. This gives you a rough measure of a person's or animal's stride.

When you can't see the next print clearly, lay the stick on the ground to work out more or less where it should be.

Jamie looked at his watch. "Only 20 minutes. We need to wait for another 10 before we can go."

They spent the next 10 minutes looking carefully around the camp, to see if any animals had passed by in the night.

"Here's a track!" shouted Ed. "Squirrel!"

Jamie went over to take a look. There was a muddy patch near the side of Sam's tent, with little foot-prints leading over it. "I've never seen squirrel tracks as clear as that before," Jamie said. He got out his note pad and made a quick drawing of the tracks, trying to copy them the right size.

Then he put his pad away and looked at his watch again. "OK. It's well over half an hour now. We can go."

They set off, following Sam's trail.

Chapter 3
Stalking

They walked slowly and in silence, the way that Sam had taught them, stepping on the outside of their feet before rolling the rest of the foot down. The idea was to melt into the woods, the way all the animals did. Humans tend to make far too much noise. In fact, when they stood still, they could hear shouts and bangs, way over to the other side of the woods.

STALKING TIPS

Test the ground before you put your foot down. If you feel a twig that might snap, lift your foot again and place it somewhere else.

Don't go anywhere in a hurry. Move very slowly, one step at a time.

Once you are close to the thing you are creeping up on, you could go down on your hands and knees or even crawl. You will find it easier to stay still if you need to, and you are less likely to be seen.

"Pssst!"

"What is it?" said Jamie in a whisper.

"Badger." Ed pointed down at a big roundish paw print. You could hardly see it, but it was close to a fallen-down branch. If the badger had passed this way, it would have brushed against the branch. Jamie kneeled down to look at it more closely.

"Hairs!" he muttered. "Look."

There were two black-and-white hairs stuck to the underside of the branch.

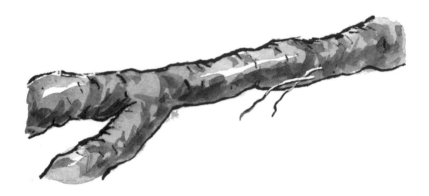

The boys looked around. Now they knew a badger had passed close by, it was easy to see where he'd gone. His snuffling nose had turned lots of leaves over making a trail right across the forest floor.

They picked up Sam's trail again, and carried on. They often played this game with Sam. He made it a bit easier for them by making a clear foot-print every now and again. Otherwise, it would be tricky to follow his tracks very far.

They passed an old dead tree trunk, lying flat on the ground. Jamie spotted something on it, and went over for a closer look.

"It's an owl pellet," he said. "Maybe it was coughed up by that barn owl we saw last night."

PELLETS

Pellets are made of food that a bird can't digest - for example, fur, feathers and bones. Birds of prey cough them up, and so do crows and gulls. You can tell which bird a pellet belongs to by its shape, its colour and what's inside it.

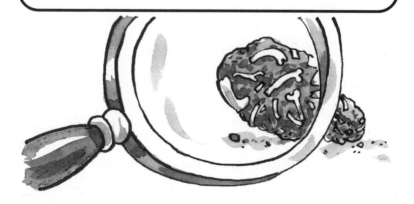

Ed poked the object with his tracking stick. It was in the shape of a little solid tube, a grey colour, with bits of fur and feather sticking out of it. It fell apart, and they got their magnifying glasses out.

"There's a bit of bird's skull," said Jamie. "It's the beak."

"Yeah. So the owl ate a bird," agreed Ed. "But it must have eaten something furry, too."

"Maybe a shrew. Look, here's a jaw-bone."

They looked at the tiny bits of bone for a few moments. Then Jamie got to his feet. "We'd better get on," he said. "We'll never find Sam before lunch at this rate."

****

DIFFERENT OWL PELLETS

Ed and Jamie have made a mistake about the pellet they've found. Barn owls don't tend to eat other birds. They mostly eat little mammals, so their pellets only have fur in them, not feathers. And their pellets are round, not like a tube.

They've found a tawny owl's pellet.

But they'd only gone a few more steps when they spotted something else. It was Jamie who saw it first. "Look at this!" he yelled. He was so excited he completely forgot to stay quiet. "It's some kind of deer!"

"That's really odd," Ed said. "It's not like any of the deer tracks that Sam's shown us."

Jamie looked at the tracks. They were about the same size as a fallow deer's hoof prints, or maybe a female red deer. But the shape was a bit odd. Rather than two little oval prints, side by side, they were kind of flat at the bottom – and there were two other little dents in the ground behind each print.

"We've got to follow it," said Jamie.

Ed wasn't sure. "What about tracking Sam?" he asked. "We'll lose his trail."

"Never mind about that. We'll find it again, easy," said Jamie. He sounded more confident than he felt, but he was much too excited to care. "We'll follow our own tracks back to this spot."

Ed looked down at the strange hoof print. "OK," he said. He grinned at Jamie. "You're right. Let's go."

It was an easy trail to follow. The creature, whatever it was, must have been heavy – its hooves had sunk deep into the soft ground. Jamie laid down his tracking stick to measure how big its strides were, but he didn't really need to. They had no problem spotting where the next print was.

"Here's another print – and another," gasped Ed, starting to jog.

"Slow down," said Jamie. He dropped his voice to a whisper. "We want to find it, remember. So we mustn't let it know we're coming."

Making as little noise as possible, they began to creep forward. In this part of the wood there were a lot of bushes, and the animal's trail wound in and out of them. Jamie and Ed kept their heads down, trying to focus hard on all the clues.

Suddenly, Jamie heard a noise. He looked up. "What's that?"

Ed didn't have time to answer. One of the bushes nearby seemed to be coming alive! It was rustling and shaking like crazy.

Then something huge and brown charged out of it. Huge and brown and coming right at them!

Jamie's heart started to pound in terror. All he could see were horrible piggy eyes and snapping jaws – and tusks.

"Run!" he yelled.

He didn't need to. Ed had already taken off, running away as fast as his legs would carry him.

Chapter 4
The Chase

"It's going to get us!" panted Ed.

They were still running flat out, jumping over fallen tree trunks, ducking under branches, and trying to dodge in and out of gaps between the bushes.

"Just – keep – going!" shouted Jamie. He didn't have enough breath to say anything else. His lungs were killing him and his legs felt as though they were about to collapse.

All he could hear were his feet thumping on the ground, and horrible snarling sounds behind him.

On and on they went. Jamie dropped his tracking stick, but he wasn't going to stop to pick it up, that was sure! Then, just when he thought he couldn't run another step, Ed looked behind them.

"It's gone," he gasped.

The creature had vanished. The two boys stopped running. Jamie leaned against a tree trunk, totally out of breath. His chest hurt. In fact he hurt all over. He couldn't speak for a few moments. All he could do was gulp in air, like a fish when it's out of water.

"What ... on earth ... was that?" asked Ed.

Jamie took a deep breath in through his nose. He still felt shaky. "Wild boar," he said.

"Wild what?"

"Wild boar," repeated Jamie. Now he came to think about it, he'd read something about them in a newspaper, not long ago.

"But they don't live in Britain," said Ed.

Jamie nodded. "Oh yes, they do. There are lots of them. And that must have been one of the biggest!"

WILD BOAR IN BRITAIN

Although wild boar were all killed about three hundred years ago, they are slowly making the British country-side their home again. This has happened as a result of them escaping from farms. They have now been spotted in many places across the UK, but they are most common in the south of England and parts of Wales.

Once they'd got their breath back, the boys stood and listened. The woods seemed quiet. They weren't sure when the boar had stopped chasing them, but it was nowhere to be seen. A robin chirped at them from a nearby branch, and they heard the 'dddrrrrrrrrr' of a woodpecker drumming on a tree trunk. It just seemed like a normal, quiet day again. Jamie began to wonder if the chase had happened at all – but then he tried moving his legs. They still hurt like crazy. The chase had happened, all right.

WOODPECKERS

You can sometimes attract a woodpecker by knocking on a tree trunk with a stone to make a 'tap-tap' sound. The woodpecker will think you have found a good feeding site, and will come to check it out.

Ed looked at his watch. "It's already 11 o'clock," he said. "And now we're really lost."

Jamie sighed. It was true. Sure, they could follow their tracks back to where they'd been before – but they both knew what that could mean. They might bump into the not-so-friendly boar again.

"There's no point in trying to find Sam," said Ed. "There's no way we can find our way back to his trail."

"No," agreed Jamie. "I reckon we should try to find our way back to camp. Sam will come and find us in the end."

"Yeah," said Ed. "In the end."

Chapter 5
Lost

"Let's go," said Ed. His face was pale. "We'll have to walk slowly. I twisted my ankle, jumping over one of those tree trunks."

Jamie got out his compass, but he knew it wouldn't be much use. The problem was, they didn't know which way they'd run when they'd been chased. And they'd been so busy looking at tracks before, that they had forgotten to check their direction. They'd probably come more or less north-west. But only more or less. So now they should go south-east, and hope for the best.

They set off. Ed was limping, and they were both feeling nervous. Every time something rustled in the bushes, they jumped.

But as they walked, Jamie remembered more of what he'd read in the newspaper.

"They were extinct here," he told Ed. "Wild boar, that is. They died out about 300 years ago. But people have started farming them, and quite a lot have escaped. They're breeding like crazy now, all over the UK."

"Well, they're crazy all right," muttered Ed.

"They can grow pretty big," Jamie went on. "But I don't understand why it attacked us. The newspaper said they were shy."

"Shy!" Ed snorted. "That's a good one, Jamie."

"Yeah. And you don't tend to see them during the day, either. They're supposed to be nocturnal – you know, active at night."

"Well, they got it all wrong, wrong, wrong," said Ed. "They're wild snarling monsters that leap out at you in broad day-light!"

WILD BOAR LIFESTYLE

Wild boar are 'omnivorous', which means that they eat both plants and meat. But most of their diet is vegetarian, and they don't hunt anything big – they just eat little animals like mice and lizards, and also worms and grubs that they find in the soil. But they will gladly eat any meat that they find (this is called 'scavenging').

Ed and Jamie set off. They tried to avoid the bushes, but before long, there seemed to be bushes all round them. They stopped. A squirrel scampered up a nearby tree and chittered down at them.

"Now what?" asked Ed. "Let's face it, Jamie. We're still lost, and that beast must still be hiding in wait for us somewhere."

DO WILD BOARS ATTACK PEOPLE?

Boars tend to be active at night ('nocturnal'). In the day, they stay hidden under bushes to rest. They have been known to attack dogs and people, but only when they feel under threat. And a female wild boar will attack to protect her piglets. So although they are not usually a danger to humans, it's best not to disturb them.

Jamie sat down on a fallen-down tree trunk. "We need to think," he said.

Ed sat down next to him with a sigh. "Maybe we're going in circles," he said.

Both boys knew that people who were lost nearly always walked in circles. That was why it was important to stay in one place, if you were hoping that someone would come and find you. But Ed and Jamie had a compass – so they should be keeping to a straight line, more or less.

Jamie peered at the compass. "I don't think we are. We're still going south-east. Trouble is, we could have gone straight past the camp without seeing it."

He stared down at the ground, thinking through everything that Sam had ever told them. Don't panic. Stay calm. That was what Sam was always saying. If you're in a panic, you can't think straight. His eye drifted over the ground by his feet. They needed a clue. Something. Anything –

"What's that?" said Ed suddenly.

"What?"

Ed pointed. "That." There was something shiny on the ground, almost hidden by leaves. He got up, and picked it up. It was a small, square silver thing with patterns carved all over it.

"It's Sam's lighter!" exclaimed Jamie. He grinned in relief. "He must have passed this way."

Ed nodded. "Let's look for tracks!"

They began to search the area around the tree trunk, hunting for foot-prints. It was difficult, because the ground was covered in leaves. But they knew the signs to look out for – leaves that had been pressed flat, or that had been turned over to show their wet under-sides.

"Here!" called Jamie. "I've found a print!"

Ed went over. Both boys stared down at the clear shape of a boot, pressed onto the leaves.

"He went that way!" cried Ed, pointing through the bushes. "Let's go!"

But they had only followed the trail for a few steps when they came across another trail. This time, it wasn't Sam's. In fact, it wasn't human at all. It was the same as the strange tracks they'd followed before.

"The wild boar," Jamie said in a whisper.

And then, with a trembling finger, Ed pointed at something else. There were splashes of something on the ground, and on some low-lying branches. It was still wet, and it glistened where the sun shone on it.

It was blood.

Chapter 6
Found!

Now that they'd spotted one splash of blood, they began to see more. There was a clear trail of it, all mixed in with the human foot-prints and the tracks of the boar.

"It must have got him," muttered Ed. "It must have attacked him."

"We have to follow, and look for Sam," said Jamie. "He needs our help."

Ed looked scared. "If we follow the trail, we might meet the boar again. Then what will we do?" He stopped. "Maybe we should go and get help instead."

"Get help? Where from?" asked Jamie. "We're lost, remember."

Ed looked round. A cloud had passed over the sun, and the woods seemed darker and more gloomy. "Well, I don't fancy tracking an angry boar, that's all."

"Neither do I," said Jamie. "But Sam must be badly hurt, or he wouldn't be bleeding so much. The boar must have gored him with its tusks, then chased him through the woods. Maybe that's why he dropped his lighter."

"At least he can still run," Ed pointed out. "He can't be hurt that badly, or he'd be lying somewhere near here."

"Yes, but how long can he carry on?" asked Jamie. "He won't be able to keep going forever. And maybe he can't run very fast. We have to find him, before ... before ..."

He couldn't finish. The boys looked at each other. It was too horrible to think about what they might find if the boar had caught Sam again.

Ed took a deep breath. "OK. You're right," he said. "We have to find him. Standing here is a waste of time."

Feeling jumpy, the boys started following the trail. They moved as quickly as they dared, making as little noise as possible. Every few moments, they stopped to listen, but all they could hear were birds calling. Sometimes, they spotted badger tracks and deer tracks, and they even spotted the pale, twisted scat of a fox on a tree stump. But they didn't stop. They kept their eyes on the main trail.

CARNIVORE SCAT

Carnivores are animals that eat other animals, and you can find out a lot about their diet from their scat – or poo. Fox scat often looks white, because foxes eat so many bones. Some carnivores, including foxes, leave their scat in places where other foxes will notice it, such as on tree stumps. This way, they mark out their territory, and warn other foxes to keep away.

"At least this is an easy trail to follow," said Jamie in a whisper. "Much easier than just following Sam."

"Yeah, I guess –" began Ed. Then he stopped suddenly. He grabbed Jamie's arm and gripped it hard. "Look. There. Under those bushes."

Jamie saw where he was pointing, and stared. There was something big, brown and hairy lying in a patch of bushes.

The wild boar.

Both boys stood very, very still. Jamie could feel his heart beating in his chest.

"Let's back away," he said. His voice was full of fear. "We mustn't let it hear us."

Quietly, and slowly, they took a few steps backwards.

"It's not moving," muttered Ed. "Do you think it's dead?"

Jamie peered at the brown side of the boar, which seemed to be moving up and down, ever so slightly. "I think I can see it breathing. Maybe we should take a closer look at it."

"Are you kidding?" Ed rolled his eyes.

Just then, the boar moved one of its back legs.

"No, OK, you're right," agreed Jamie quickly. "We can look at it through binoculars in a moment. Let's keep away from it for now."

They began to tip-toe backwards, and then round the patch of bushes where the boar was lying. Ed led the way, and they moved very, very slowly, picking up one foot at a time and putting it down softly. They didn't want to rustle any leaves or snap any twigs.

When Jamie felt something land on his shoulder, he thought he would die of fright.

"ARRGH!" Jamie yelped. He just couldn't help it.

Ed spun around, a finger to his lips. Then his mouth dropped open in surprise.

"Sam!" he gasped.

Chapter 7
End of the Hunt

Sam looked at his watch. "12:40 pm," he said. "That's good going, boys. Well done."

Jamie and Ed stared at him. Sam had a big smile on his face, and didn't look hurt at all. "But …" stuttered Jamie. "You haven't got any blood on you."

"We thought the boar had got you," said Ed.

"We were really worried!" added Jamie. "It charged us in the woods. Then we tried to find our way back to camp, but we found your lighter and all the tracks. We thought you were really hurt."

Sam shook his head. "It's not me who's hurt," he said. His voice sounded sad. "A boar wouldn't charge humans without a good reason. They're shy, nocturnal creatures."

Ed and Jamie looked at each other. That was what the newspaper had said, too!

"So what's happened to it?" asked Jamie. He looked over at the boar.

"Come and see," said Sam.

"No way!" Ed shook his head. "I'm not getting anywhere near it."

"Don't worry," said Sam. "This boar won't be getting up again, I'm afraid."

They crept forward until they could see the boar more clearly. Its sides were still moving up and down, but only just. Sam led them around to take a look at its head. Now they could see that blood and foam flecked its tusks and muzzle, and that its piggy eyes were half-closed.

Sam pointed. "It's been shot," he said. "Look at its chest."

The dark bristles of the boar's coat were clogged with blood.

"So is that why it charged at us?" asked Jamie.

Sam nodded. "Yes. It was hit, but the bullet missed its heart. So it went rampaging through the woods – and found you."

BOAR FAMILY HABITS

Boars usually live in groups, but the groups are made up of females, piglets and young boars. The male boars tend to live on their own, unless it's the mating period. Then they hunt out the groups of females to breed.

Wild boars are a rich brown colour, but wild boar piglets are covered in brown and cream stripes.

"Poor thing." Jamie bent over the boar, and studied its big muscular chest and scary tusks. The tusks didn't seem so big, close up. He felt sorry for the boar now.

"Yes." Sam sighed. "Farmers don't like them, that's the problem. And of course, wild boar is very tasty meat, too."

"So where are the hunters now?" asked Ed.

Sam grinned. "Oh, I expect they're somewhere on the other side of the woods," he said.

"Something tells me you've seen them," said Jamie.

"Yes. When I left you, I was about half an hour away from the camp when I heard people shouting and firing shots. I wanted to see what was going on, so I walked towards all the noise. I began to see lots of wild boar tracks along the way."

"We were following wild boar tracks when we got charged," Jamie told him.

"Well, there are plenty of them," said Sam. "All of a sudden, a big male boar came crashing through the woods. It didn't see me, but I could see that it had been shot. I watched it charge off into the bushes, then I waited for the hunters to arrive."

"And they went off in the wrong direction?" Jamie guessed.

Sam nodded. "They weren't even following the tracks properly – they just shouted, 'Which way did it go?' So I told them. They set off again, and I followed a little way behind. Before long they were following a different set of tracks altogether."

Ed and Jamie shook their heads. It was amazing how bad some people were at tracking.

"They didn't even think to follow the trail of blood instead," Sam carried on. "Anyway, I followed the trail myself."

"And in the meantime, the boar must have found us," said Ed.

"Yes. I came across your tracks, too," said Sam. "But I could tell it hadn't caught you. So I thought I would keep on following the boar until it collapsed."

"How much longer do you think it will live?" asked Ed.

All three of them looked at the boar. It was now completely still. Sam leaned down and looked at it closely. "It's already dead," he said in a quiet voice.

"So now what do we do?" asked Jamie. "We can't move it, can we?"

Sam shook his head. "No way," he said. "It's a fully grown male – much too heavy for us to lift. We'll just leave it. The hunters will find it in the end. At least it's had the chance to die in peace."

The sun had come out again, casting shadows on the boar's back. Ed and Jamie took a last look at its gleaming tusks, and Jamie made a quick drawing of them in his notepad. It was a sight that he knew he wouldn't forget in a hurry.

Then Sam picked up his bag. "Come on," he said. "We've still got the afternoon left to do a lot more tracking. Let's go and eat our lunch."

AUTHOR FACT FILE
GILL HARVEY

Who would be your ideal camping partner?
Anyone who can laugh when things go wrong!
(And make me laugh too).

Where would you most like to explore?
I'm in the process of exploring Africa, where
I often camp, and I've still got a LOT to see.

What's your favourite campfire food?
Marshmallows, of course!

What's your favourite forest animal?
Chimpanzees.

If you could track any animal, what would it be?
A leopard.

**Which animal would you least like to be woken by
in the middle of the night?**
A hyena. They bite people's faces off.

ILLUSTRATOR FACT FILE
MARTIN REMPHRY

Who would be your ideal camping partner?
A chef. He could do all the cooking!

Where would you most like to explore?
A Transylvanian forest, searching for
werewolves.

What's your favourite campfire food?
Sausages.

If you could track any animal, what would it be?
An elephant's foot prints would be easy to follow,
but you would have to be careful of the
droppings.

**Which animal would you least like to be woken
by in the middle of the night?**
A wolf, or even a werewolf would be scary, but
on a hot summer's night a whining mosquito can
drive me insane!

Barrington Stoke would like to thank all its readers for commenting on the manuscript before publication and in particular:

Laila Ahmed

Caoimhe Brady

Will Butterworth

Jean Button

Theresa Collins

Anna Dawson

Phillip Dawson

Aaliyah Ifrah Haji

Lara Hamandi

Chelsea Hanney

Jasotharan Haridas

Cassie Heathcote

Aisling Kealy

Graham Littler

Julia Littler

Catherine McAlpine

Lisa M'Donagh

Ann Molumby

Freya O'Connell

Ryan O'Sullivan

Rachel Siddique

Oliver Simmons

Bilan Sulob

Tom Wilcox

Become a Consultant!

Would you like to give us feedback on our titles before they are published? Contact us at the email address below – we'd love to hear from you!

info@barringtonstoke.co.uk
www.barringtonstoke.co.uk